Contents

William Collins' dream of knowledge for all began with the publication of his first book in 1819.
A self-educated mill worker, he not only enriched millions of lives, but also founded a flourishing publishing house.
Today, staying true to this spirit, Collins books are packed with inspiration, innovation and practical expertise.
They place you at the centre of a world of possibility and give you exactly what you need to explore it.

Collins. Freedom to teach.

Published by Collins
An imprint of HarperCollins*Publishers*
The News Building, 1 London Bridge Street, London, SE1 9GF, UK

HarperCollins Publishers
1st Floor, Watermarque Building, Ringsend Road, Dublin 4, Ireland

Browse the complete Collins catalogue at
www.collins.co.uk

British Library Cataloguing-in-Publication Data
A catalogue record for this publication is available from the British Library.

Compiled by: Fiona Macgregor
Publisher: Elaine Higgleton
Product manager: Letitia Luff
Commissioning editor: Rachel Houghton
Edited by: Hannah Hirst-Dunton
Editorial management: Oriel Square
Cover designer: Kevin Robbins
Cover illustrations: Jouve India Pvt. Ltd.
Additional text credit: p 3–8, 18–21, 30–31 Fiona Macgregor
p 9–13 Angie Belcher, p 22–29 Robyn Lever
Internal illustrations: p 2–8 Sahitya Rani, p 9–17 Sylwia Filipczak, p 18–21 Angeles Peinador, p 22–29 Tomislav Zlatic
Typesetter: Jouve India Pvt. Ltd.
Production controller: Lyndsey Rogers
Printed and Bound in the UK using 100% Renewable Electricity at Martins the Printers

MIX
Paper from
responsible sources
FSC www.fsc.org **FSC™ C007454**

This book is produced from independently certified FSC™ paper to ensure responsible forest management.

For more information visit:
www.harpercollins.co.uk/green

Acknowledgements

With thanks to all the kindergarten staff and their schools around the world who have helped with the development of this course, by sharing insights and commenting on and testing sample materials:

Calcutta International School: Sharmila Majumdar, Mrs Pratima Nayar, Preeti Roychoudhury, Tinku Yadav, Lakshmi Khanna, Mousumi Guha, Radhika Dhanuka, Archana Tiwari, Urmita Das; Gateway College (Sri Lanka): Kousala Benedict; Hawar International School: Kareen Barakat, Shahla Mohammed, Jennah Hussain; Manthan International School: Shalini Reddy; Monterey Pre-Primary: Adina Oram; Prometheus School: Aneesha Sahni, Deepa Nanda; Pragyanam School: Monika Sachdev; Rosary Sisters High School: Samar Sabat, Sireen Freij, Hiba Mousa; Solitaire Global School: Devi Nimmagadda; United Charter Schools (UCS): Tabassum Murtaza and staff; Vietnam Australia International School: Holly Simpson

The publishers wish to thank the following for permission to reproduce photographs.

(t = top, c = centre, b = bottom, r = right, l = left)

p 30tl kazoka/Shutterstock, p 30tr bluedog studio/Shutterstock, p 30bl Romolo Tavani/Shutterstock, p 30br Fotokostic/Shutterstock, p 31t lovelyday12/Shutterstock, p 31b Valentina Razumova/Shutterstock

The publishers gratefully acknowledge the permission granted to reproduce the copyright material in this book. Every effort has been made to trace copyright holders and to obtain their permission for the use of copyright material. The publishers will gladly receive any information enabling them to rectify any error or omission at the first opportunity.

Extracts from Collins Big Cat readers reprinted by permission of HarperCollins *Publishers* Ltd

All © HarperCollins*Publishers*

I am Sam

I am Sam.

I paint me.

eyes

hair

ears

nose

mouth

I am Sam.

I paint me!

eyes

hair

ears

nose

mouth

Six of us

I am Dan.

This is Mum.

She can fix things.

This is Gran.

She chops the chicken.

This is Jen.

She sings to Bub.

This is Dad.

He has figs. Yum!

My senses

I see with my eyes.
I smell with my nose.

I hear with my ears.
I wriggle my toes.

I taste with my mouth.
I touch with my hand.

A lovely day in the
waves and the sand.

Pam naps

Pam naps.

Dan, Tim and Sam sit.

Dan nips Tim.

Pam naps.

Sam drinks from a tap.

Pam naps.

Dan sits on a pan.

Pam pats the cats.

The cats nap.

Grow, plant, grow!

seed

soil

sun

water

Grow, plant, grow!

Reading notes

Story	Sounds	Language structures
I am Sam	'a'	Answering questions: *I am...*
Six of us	'a' 'm' 'i'	Saying who someone is: *This is...*
My senses	's' 'm' 'e'	Identifying what you see or smell: *I see, I smell*
Pam naps	'p' 'n' 't'	Making short 2- and 3-letter words: *am, Sam, pat*
Grow, plant, grow!	's' 'p' 'd'	Talking about plants; use the words sun, soil, plant, water

When you read these stories to your children at home, point out the new sound(s) in each story. Ask: *What sound is this? What letter is this?* Encourage your child to find the letter on the page. Then get them to say the sound, and the word, out loud.

Practise these language structures by asking questions. For example, ask: *Who are you?* to elicit the response: *I am (name)*; or ask: *Who is this?* to get the answer: *This is Dad.*